#GirlRogues

braggadocio

ZIZZI BONAH

Published by

She And The Cat's Mother

Published by She And The Cat's Mother 2016
SheAndTheCatsMother.com

Copyright Zizzi Bonah 2016
All rights reserved
Zizzi Bonah is the pseudonym of Ida Barker
Picture of Zizzi on book's cover by She And The Cat's Mother 2023

Lyrics from the song 'Push the Cow over the Moon' written by Ida Barker. Copyright 2009 Beatroute Records International. IdaBarker.live

All characters in this publication are fictitious and any resemblance to real persons, living or dead, is purely coincidental. This book is sold subject to the condition that it shall not, by way of trade or otherwise, be lent, re-sold, hired out or otherwise circulated without the publisher's prior consent in any form of binding or cover other than that in which it is published and without a similar condition including this condition being imposed on the subsequent purchaser.

A CIP catalogue record for this book is available from the British Library.

Paperback ISBN: 9780993552762
eBook ISBN: 9780993552779

Dedication:
To girls with rogue tendencies

:

CONTENTS

:

Zizzi Bonah's collection of fantasy noir short stories and verses are for those with minds as broad as braggadocio, and nerves hard enough to rival a diamond from the first water. #GirlRogues are dangerous to love, more dangerous to ignore – which girl are you?

HEALTH WARNING: This book is rather like surviving your renegade's cooking, and should therefore be taken in small bites. For that reason, it comes with no letter of recommendation!

#GIRLROGUE STATEMENT

"Braggadocio..."

#GirlRogue

_____Statement_____

:

I hereby proclaim the intent – along with all female rogues – to devote my time in the pursuit of trusting my own instincts, and in doing so, learn to take chances and responsibilities on my own footing. For I uphold the right to stand for something; rather than falling for anything.

As I give mind to the next wave of future to sweep around my feet – my only alibi is the beachy sands (should saltwater get in my eyes), as I learn which rules to follow, and which rules to break. And in doing so, maximise my good, bad and virtuoso qualities, with the aim to gain a lifetime membership within: #GirlRogues' Society.

1) A #GirlRogue should never self-sabotage or reject herself by doubting her own capabilities. She must find a way to make her choices count, instead of counting them against herself.

Remember: A #GirlRogue learns more from one mistake than ever she does from a success.

2) A #GirlRogue isn't reckless enough to wish – wishing is an empty emotion. Instead she plots and plans to bring about her own opportunities, in order to be where she wants to be –

3) A #GirlRogue wilfully adopts the strategy to take care of herself; for how can she expect someone else to have her best interests at heart, if she doesn't already? Think: self!

4) A #GirlRogue should learn to become her own best friend, (after all, she's the one living full-time in her life), for there are few rescuers – but for those who rescue themselves – there is laughter in the dark.

Above all, a #GirlRogue is free to disregard this statement in favour of assembling her own rules to live by – while carrying forward the motto:

> *"Faith is a handrail, not a prison, but somethings get lost in translation. Sometimes women talk, for the same reasons men don't, but from the inside looking out, the sky won't fall in."*

> ___An honouree #GirlRogue Z.B___

MISS MANNERS AND MIRTH CONTROL

"Word-corpse poetry…"

Miss Manners and Mirth Control

:

Miss Manners was of the standing,

To adhere by the book.

She dwelt in a place where,

Correct was the rule.

No exception to her mind,

Would be tolerated.

Words must know their place,

With grammar and punctuation.

:

As a person born into,

The element of earth.

With a dominant nature,

Governed by nurture.

Miss Manners nurtured words,

Which pressed upon her page.

As a ritual,

Every season she'd engage.

:

To let the words run loose,

To dance across the page.

She'd pepper grammar here 'n there,

Adding a pinch of worth.

"My little darlings" she'd say,

"Uphold the tradition.
Gift me the winner's prize,
At the poet competition."
:

But contrary to tradition,
She failed to alight.
Miss Manners came away,
With no poet winner's prize.
Disbelief cast a shadow.
She didn't even list,
First, second or third.
Instead she was dismissed!
:

Fury and Seth,
Came to turn her spinner's wheel.
How could she not have won –
The poetry season shield?
Good manners unravelled,
From her nature of nurture.
She vowed there and then,
Over-nurture is to smother.
:

So come the next season,
Miss Manners let loose,
Words across the page,
They danced to her new tune.

"Oh my ickle darnings.
Oh my ickle werdz.
Mudder must smudder,
Wules and wegulations!"
:

Words jumped across the page,
With unnerving fright.
At sounds they'd never known,
From her well-mannered mouth.
Some words gave a banshee scream.
Others tried to flee.
But none could escape,
The page boundaries.
:

"Dimnation! Exation!
Handwrotten off their nutes!"
Miss Manners brought down her pen,
And axed their perfect snoods.
Others lost their tails.
Even fingers were not safe.
Five syllabic words,
Found themselves cut down to waif.
:

"She's a word-murderer!"
Chorused the poet society.
"I know! I know! This is the death –

Word-corpse poetry!"
"What shall we do? How do we deal —
With such a personage?"
"Off with her hands, I suggest,
She has no manners to boot!"
:

"No manners! No manners!
She's forsaken all her manners.
Off with her hands, we all suggest,
Penning a word-corpse poem!"
:

"We'll have to set example,"
Said the Judge of Ample-Pry.
"Against abstract thinking,
Or she'll set a tread sky-high."
"Guards! Guards!" called out,
The poet society.
"Take this violator.
Throw away the key!
:

"Throw away. Throw away.
Throw away the key!
Take this violator, and,
Throw away the key!"
:

"What of the competition?"

Miss Manners wrestled free.
"Have I won the season's prize?
Winner of the shield?"
"In fact" said a voice,
"I found it quite refreshing,
Miss Manners' piece didn't use,
Distraction of meaning."
:

"But" cried remnant words,
Laid strewed across the page.
"Miss Manners ought to be in jail:
A word-murdered: wholesale!"
:

"And she will" said Head Judge,
Of the poet society.
"But first the pressing issue of,
Naming the winning piece.
This season's prize goes to,
Miss Manners' masterpiece.
And a prescription of Mirth Control,
Until deceased!"

KAJAGAAGAA

(MISS RED: AN EYE FOR A TREASURE)

"Passion can be blinding, but heat is a real eye opener..."

:

Kajagaagaa

(Miss Red: An Eye For A Treasure)

:

After being out bid on every lot she had meticulously eyed-up at the Kismet Auction House, Miss Red made her way empty-handed from the premises and across the car park.

That blasted, Isobel Rupla she thought, sometimes I swear that woman seeks pleasure from outshining my finances. By rule of practice, Miss Red pulled out a bright red lipstick from her purse, and applied numerous coats of gloss to her discontented mouth, until she blazed brilliantly.

Then, centring herself, she rearranged her face at the sight of an elderly couple making their way towards her in the searing heat. She noticed the woman clutched an old battered cardboard box, while the man, holding a Kismet Auction House pamphlet, waved it briskly in the air to draw Miss Red closer.

"Main entrance to the auction house?" called the man.

"Off by the road." She snapped shut her purse with finality. "You'll have to wait however, the auction's in full flow."

The woman looked disappointed. "We were hoping

for a quick estimate before the train leaves."

"No mind, dear." The man took a handkerchief out from his trouser pocket and began to wipe his hot face and neck. "We'll just have to make a special journey."

"But we've come all this way," the woman appealed.

Miss Red scrutinised the cardboard box, the faded advertisement on the sides read: Sunflash Soap Flakes. There was no indication as to what it currently concealed. Maybe a rare Periwinkle plate or a Rhode-Island vase, or even a Catkin set... oh she prayed it would be something of the kind as her imagination unravelled at the heightened possibilities. And so, with Miss Red's curiosity spiked, she inclined her head in a beautiful gesture. "Maybe I can help?" The woman tightened her arthritic grip on the box, and Miss Red could see she needed a nudge in the right direction. "Just think of it as living a solution not a problem."

How many times, Miss Red didn't care to remember, had she seen possibilities of treasure that turned out to be nothing more than claptrap. But her joined up thinking told her, maybe, just maybe there was something to be had in this cardboard box. Something that could turn her fortune round, by purchasing it before this elderly couple made a return visit and entered the revolving auction house doors –

missing Isobel Rupla's perceptible gaze altogether.

"Do you have experience in these sorts of things?" asked the woman.

Miss Red felt an exaggeration to the facts overcoming her as she pushed back her blazing red bouffant to see them all the better. "I've been in the dealer trade for some time with all sorts of—"

"Well, we have come a long way," said the man as he replaced the damp handkerchief into his pocket. "Why not indulge?"

The woman gave a reluctant sigh, then began to open the over-used cardboard box.

Rapidly blinking, Miss Red peered into the box's depths, only to find the greeting close to a let-down as tens, maybe even hundreds of glassy false eyes glinted at her in the blazing sola sunshine. She swayed at the grotesqueness of it all...

"I do believe there's a shade of colour to match any person's eye," the woman said proudly as she began to rake her swollen fingers through the assortment of false eyes.

Miss Red couldn't bring herself to vocalise a worthy comment through her brilliant red mouth, which quickly slid sideways as her pupils narrowed independently from each other... Then, something different rose to the surface amongst the movement caused by the old woman. Amongst the glass eyes in the top left corner, a glittering red sapphire set in a gold ring caught her attention.

Miss Red's heart suddenly began to pound faster until she felt quite giddy and light-headed. For she was a Blazonard – one born into the element of fire – whose temperament was ruled by two dominant forces: passion and impatience. And as every true Blazonard knew, jewellery is an artistic medium – to be used as a language for expressing many things, and an abundance ring was the pinnacle of artistic expression.

Miss Red couldn't take her eyes off the domed red sapphire, she noted it was carved and painted from deep behind the gemstone, giving depth to the reliefs and creating the most amazing three-dimensional scene of a fire landscape: the City of Passion, in miniature.

Her mind flashed to Isobel Rupal, she'd insight a bidding war at the Kismet Auction House over this article amongst the other dealers – forcing out Miss Red's chances of affording this scintillating red sapphire of the past, never to be attained into her own future – but all she could say to herself was, I've got to have it! I've simply got to have it! I've been playing by the rules, or at least some of them for most of my life, and it hasn't got me any distance at all.

Under hooded eyes Miss Red looked at the elderly couple. Clearly they had no inclination as to how much this box of contents was really worth…

"I'll buy it!"

"We only want an estimate," said the man.

"Oh, at your age you don't want to be lugging this all the way back to the train station, and in this heat. The temperature's enough to set your hair on fire." She smiled through barred white teeth.

"That's very thoughtful of you my dear," said the woman. "But how much are you willing to pay for the eyes?"

"Try me." Miss Red held her nerve and swallowed her excitement.

The woman thought for a moment. "The price of a return train ticket?"

"That's no way to bargain," said the man. "How about two return train tickets?"

"Sold!" Miss Red swiftly opened her purse and handed over a note in one clean motion, while taking hold of the box with the other. And as Miss Red strode away with extra vigour she thought, for once in my life I'm ahead of the game. My luck has changed. Oh, if only Isobel Rupal could see me now, I'm sure she'd never, ever, sleep again!

:

The taxi pulled up in front of popular restaurant, Nexus. Miss Red's latest male conquest, Kiln paid the driver as Miss Red stepped out onto the pavement, feeling the day's heat transmit from the concrete slabs and through the soles of her shoes. Turning back to look at Kiln's shock of dark hair and brooding manner, it occurred to her how his face never much expressed his feelings, until he had been well-fed, and borderline tipsy. Or perhaps her appeal for him was fading, in light of the alluring abundance ring displayed on her finger. Her gaze rarely left it.

After the blistering heat of the streets, Nexus was like an old sin that cast a long, cold, shadow. The steel panelling re-produced some of the natural outside glare, while the rustic wooden furnishings absorbed any glimmer shines. A polite but quite determined waiter stepped forward and ushered Miss Red and Kiln to the bar – where – with pure indulgence they drank flaming red Lamborghini cocktails while waiting for a table to become vacant. Her excitement seemed to be contagious as a pressing crowd of people began to circulate round her, commenting on the breath-taking piece of jewellery she covetously wore. Yes, Miss Red was becoming quite a sensation – or rather – the ring was, and as she had attached herself to it, one came with the other.

As she continued to mentally hug herself, the first course arrived: wild tomato soup. Her mind flashed back to the box of glass eyes. She'd ditched them by Rhode-Island river on the outskirts of town. No need for them, they were virtually worthless in her opinion.

Miss Red swirled pouring-cream onto the surface of the hot soup. Then, taking her first hungry taste of the starter, she began to relax and take in its depth of savoury finesse – the subtle zingy wildness pinged on her taste buds, making her feel altogether refreshed. Keenly, Miss Red leaned forward again, lifting the spoon out of the redolent bowl towards her protruding mouth, and there, looking right at her from the soup spoon, was a roan, glass, eye!

Miss Red reeled back and screamed… the soup spoon hit the floor, but not without splattering soup all the way down her elegant dress. The roan glass eye speedily rolled beneath the table. "Kiln, that's not funny! How could you?" she demanded. Kiln looked nonplussed, she could see he didn't know what she was referring to.

The waiter hurried across to investigate the disturbance. "I'm sorry madam, what seems to be the problem?"

"There's no seems about it." Miss Red frantically shook from head to foot. "There was an eye in my soup!" She gestured beneath the table.

"An eye?!" The waiter searched. Then, reappearing, "Seems you've been mistaken, there's no eye to be seen, are you quite sure, you saw, what you think you saw?!"

"Quite!" Miss Red's voice was becoming shriller and shriller with every nuance uttered. Kiln joined in the search along with the other customers, even the restaurant manager, but no eye could be found.

"We've never had this sort of complaint before." The manager's lower lip drooped. "Perhaps you're not suited to this kind of establishment. May I suggest you go elsewhere?"

"Elsewhere?" cried Miss Red. "But it was clearly there. Right there. In my soup!"

:

Miss Red tried to put the torrid ordeal behind her. Encouraged by Kiln, together they ventured out to the cinema to see the latest production. The screen room was packed by the time they arrived. The rumbling sounds of the film trailers bombarded their senses as they jostled passed seated cinema-goers in the dimness of light. Finally, locating their seats they began to unwind, sharing a tub of popcorn. Scoop after scoop, Miss Red relished each handful of the sweet salty mix. But then, something caught her eye, something refracting the light in her hand amongst the edible treats. Miss Red sharpened her gaze in the darkened room until it became quite exact, and what she discovered was enough to turn her delicate stomach: a solid glass eye staring back at her.

Needless to say, Miss Red and Kiln where forcibly escorted off the cinema complex on the grounds of causing unnecessary chaos.

"It must be the ring!" she appealed to Kiln. "I duped the old couple into selling it for a considerable lesser price, and now, the eyes... they're watching me. Reminding me... I don't deserve to own it."

"You don't surely believe that, do you?" Kiln was matter-of-fact. "It's probably just a coincidence, nothing more. Try to forget it. I know I have."

Miss Red marginally closed her eyes on him and swallowed down her churning emotions. For her suspicions could not be quietened as easily as his. And her affirmation of guilt was to be secured by one final occurrence.

:

Escaping the heat of urban life, Miss Red trekked through the golden cornfields. Slowly she began to feel so much better about herself, "Maybe Kiln's right, maybe it's just a matter of coincidence," she reasoned. Her young heart lifted as she sighted a solitary red-alder flower swaying in the dusty breeze.

Purposefully, Miss Red made her way across and picked the large flower. Its petals felt like red velvet to her touch. "I must take it home," she told herself, "and place it in my very best Rhode-Island vase." She brought the flower closer to her flared nostrils to take in its evanescent scent, and as she peered down at this bold beauty she saw a bulbous movement – an all too familiar bulbous movement – for looming at her from the very centre of the flower head was a single, cobalt blue, glass eye.

She screamed an expletive, then dropped it at her feet and ran hell for suede all the way back home – but not before frantically searching the Rhode-Island river banks for the Sunflash Soap box she had discarded all that time ago, and which contained the mass assortment of glassy eyes.

However, to Miss Red's dismay, its whereabouts completely evaded her as she raked through the river bank foliage with her bare hands. The abrasive thorny bushes spiked her, and as she looked down at the stunning abundance ring on her finger a thought smarted her, now that she wanted nothing more than to give it away, the outcome was looking decidedly bleak in her favour, for how could she without its accompaniments – the eyes – sell it on and free herself of the consequences? This ring she once loved more than anything, or anyone, was quickly destroying her social reputation, not to mention her peace of mind.

Heavy-heartedly, Miss Red made her way up the steps to her apartment. Her mind dwelt on the elderly couple she'd duped for the ring… or had they duped her? Either way, there was no way of tracking the couple down and returning the sale to them.

Turning the key in her front door, Miss Red found the door unusually steadfast to opening, after much effort she squeezed her way through, only to discover the Sunflash cardboard box wedged behind the door. A mixture of relief and dread coursed through her veins. Relief that now she could part from the ring, but a chilling dread at the sight of the amassed glassy eyes – for they had found her – no-one, not even Kiln knew where Miss Red had abandoned the Sunflash box. It was as if the glassy eyes knew she was now ready to give up rogue ownership of the abundance ring, and so they had turned enablers, enabling her to pass the abundance ring to its next purchaser, rogue or not!

Without delay, Miss Red yanked at the ring on her swollen finger and threw the jewellery in the box.

:

On approach to the Kismet Auction House doors, Miss Red heard a voice call out to her, "Darling, how delightful to see you. Not given up the auction bug I see!" Isobel Rupla, she thought, you're such a bug-bearer! She could see this female was not strong where resisting pleasure was concerned. Her large eyes – which rarely missed a thing – and her pointed chin gave her face the shape of an inverted triangle. "Oh, and what have we here?" she cooed.

Miss Red's grip tightened on the old Sunflash box until her knuckles turned white. "I was hoping for a quick estimate on the contents."

"Maybe I can help?" The other inclined her head in a persuasive gesture.

As Miss Red opened the Sunflash box under a baking sola sun, she witnessed a similar reaction to her own on first sight of the shining glassy false eyes. Isobel Rupla swayed at the grotesqueness of it all…

"I do believe there is a shade of colour to match any person's eye," Miss Red said proudly as she began to rake her river silted fingers through the assortment of false eyes, while moving the abundance ring to the surface. And suddenly Isobel Rupla's mouth grew smaller, as her pupils opened wider at the sight of the domed red sapphire displaying a three-dimensional scene of a fire landscape: the City of Passion, in miniature.

"I'll buy it!"

"I only want an estimate."

"Oh, you don't want to be lugging this about in the heat. The temperature's enough to set your hair on fire." Isobel Rupla smiled through barred white teeth.

"That's very thoughtful of you, how much are you willing to pay for the eyes?"

"Try me."

Miss Red focused on Isobel, she didn't want to ask for more than she gave in case the consequences remained with her. "How about the price of a return train ticket, two fold?"

"Sold!" Isobel Rupla opened her purse and handed over a note in one clean motion, while taking hold of the box with the other. "How lucky I was to bump into you."

No, thought Miss Red, the luck was my invention.

OPTIMISM IS AN EYE DISEASE

"Tears as souvenirs..."

:

Optimism is an Eye Disease

:

Never trust an optician,

Who gazes into your eyes.

Then tells you optimism,

Is a disease of the eyes.

:

For she's the sort who'll collect,

Your tears as souvenirs.

And wallow in cries and sighs,

Of past misery and fears.

:

No, never trust an optician,

Who gazes into your eyes,

And asks for tear stained handkerchiefs,

Without batting her eyes.

:

For she'll extract salt crystals,

From your tears and use them as,

Bath salts to bathe in or,

Dash them on fish, chips and scraps.

:

No, never trust an optician,

Who gazes into your eyes,

The currency she deals in,

Tear jewels the size of pork pies.
:

For she's the sort who'll claim,
The sand got in your eyes.
Then tell you optimism,
Is a disease full of lies.

THE GIRL WHO USED UP ALL HER SMILES

"When appearance and reality are not always in harmony..."

:

The Girl Who Used Up All Her Smiles

:

The high street was washed clean by recent rainfall, and the grey skies had not yet passed to brighter ones, but this in no way dampened her spirit. Silver Dorn was a female who had new limits to conquer, or rather, new limits to con.

She walked tall with graceful strides, admiring her perfect impressions in each and every shop window. Marvelling at how she could still emanate a girlish quality, without wearing frills and furbelows.

Pushing back her gun-metal coloured hair, she remembered how, from an early age she had realised the power emitted from a smile – not only could a smile light up a face making it instantly more youthful, it also had the power to beguile others. A quality essential to Silver Dorn's recent success – selling bottled air.

In her first trial of putting the product to sale, the air trapped in each glass bottle came from the Grand Primmer motor car race, captured from the edge of the circuit track. And while her business contemporaries would say, "Who would be daft enough to sell the air we breathe, let alone buy it?" Well, plenty so it transpired. In fact, Silver Dorn found her novel idea inundated, demand out-striped supply.

As her business grew from strength to strength, she broadened the range of air products, from car racing tracks, to boxing events, book launches, concerts and everything in-between. No big event was too small an opportunity to over-look. Sales continued to expand.

With vigour, she approached the revolving doors to the building of her office headquarters. The building was a tall imposing structure, built skilfully by reinforced glass that reached into the clouded grey skies. It was by no accident, Silver Dorn had selected this building to work from. Its designer had meticulously chosen materials of high throw back qualities for the building's interior. Allowing Silver to not only admire her own image infinitely, but also enable her to shrewdly keep tabs on other people's expressions and visible reactions – through mirrors in mirrors – when they had turned their backs on her and let down their guard.

As she skirted the glass reception desk, her usual power of attraction seemed to strangely evade her. So much so, Silver Dorn couldn't help but exaggerate her character swagger, and depthless glitter of the eyes to accompany her smile. But each person she passed on route to the escalator not only gave her a double take, followed by a step backwards, she saw their faces drop with a look of... well, a look she was unfamiliar with and could only describe as… horror!

"Is that Silver Dorn?"

"She looks…"

"…different?"

"No, can't be…"

In all her seasons she had been a female who attracted, not repelled. Being born into the privileged element of metal – the self-elected fourth element – superior to all other elements; wood, fire, earth and water, this had not only reinforced her confidence about herself but also her own abilities. The two dominate forces influencing a Metalgant's character was melancholy and romance, and unusually Silver Dorn was beginning to feel quite melancholic about herself.

Quickening her step up the moving escalator, Silver made her way to the nearest mirror wall to seek out a close up to her appearance, and what she saw, shocked. She let out a sharp expel of breath as the internal and external image she had immaculately created had completely left her. Silver Dorn could, no longer, smile!

With all the will power she could muster, she fought to raise the muscles in her lower face, to lift the edges of her bowed mouth. But the more she strove, the more her pink lips made the shape of a snarl, a grimace, even a puckered up irregular sneer. And from this peculiar experience, Silver thought of herself as not only fiercely unattractive, but with it, a two syllable word sprang to mind – a word she had never identified with herself before – the word: ugly!

She raised a quivering hand across her mouth and grappled in her couture brassy handbag for her sunglasses, then circumnavigated her way to the office, bypassing her secretary's verbal memos and slammed the office door shut.

Within moments there was a tentative knock on the glass door. "Miss Dorn? Miss Dorn is anything the matter?"

Silver didn't answer, instead she edged to the office window, which served to mirror back a portrayal of herself. She raised her sunglasses to the top of her head for a clearer view and studied her unwanted transformation. Gingerly she prodded her face muscles, then attempted to physically push up a smile using both hands. But the effect was minimal as she heard the door slowly open and then click shut.

"Miss Dorn, you asked me earlier to remind you of forthcoming schedules…"

"Take a seat, Melanie," she said, not lifting her eyes to meet the girl's through the throw back. "But prepare yourself, what you are about to see isn't pretty, in fact I'd go as far to say it's pretty darn extreme!" With all her courage, Silver turned to her loyal employee, then slumped heavily onto the sumptuous leather chair, her handbag rested in her lap.

"You look so unsightly!" blurted out the figure with soft velvety eyes and long straight hair.

"Your honesty is not necessary. I'm fully aware of what I may look like. What I need to know is, how do I reinstate my healthy look of youth and beauty?"

"Well!" The girl looked bemused, then baffled, but Silver knew Melanie was not the type to pass a question by. "My hunch–"

"Oh, I do hate hunches," said Silver. "They're so condescending."

Melanie cleared her throat. "Your best bet would be to ask a Cheshire cat. They're known for their smiles. It defines their innate character. What's the well-known saying?" She paused momentarily, "Ah, yes! Grinning like a Cheshire cat."

:

Dusk was beginning to take hold on Downton Park. The occasional jogger sprinted by Silver Dorn; she pulled the cashmere scarf higher to conceal her smile-less mouth. "Melanie had better be right about this," she mumbled, and drew the long coat tighter against the cold air. She shivered and called out, "Here Kitty, Kitty. Here, Puss cat..."

In answer to her calling, she spotted an odd moggy and a long haired blue-breed, but not a Cheshire cat. With a vigilant eye to her surroundings, Silver began to rattle the small ornamental box containing plain cat biscuits for extra enticement, "Here Puss, Puss…"

"Who are you calling, Puss?" Rasped a voice high above her.

Silver condensed her eyesight in the fading light and peered into the lush tree foliage above. "Hello? I'm looking for a cat that goes by the name of Cheshire." She saw two large green eyes shining down on her, and by a swish of a furry paw, a leafy branch lifted to unveil a magnificent Cheshire cat. "I'm seeking his erudite advice?" she answered with self-evident friendliness, their paths never having crossed in business.

"Sorry, my life is fully occupied by me. I don't have time for giving advice." He leant forward from the tree branch. "Are those the best cat treats you've thought to bring with you?"

"Yes, but I could bring something else, something more to your liking if you prefer…"

He purred deeply and twitched his whiskers in a sophisticated manner. "I'm the sort of cat who's used to a much higher standard of edible treats you see. And those simply won't do my equilibrium any good. Pha,

pha. No good at all." Elegantly the feline leapt down from his position and onto a metal park bench. "Let me have a closer look at you."

With ruthless energy she came to sit next to him on the bench. He flashed her a beaming smile, and in that instance, Silver felt quite envious at the sight of such a brilliant, perfect smile – quite unlike her – envy had never been in her mind or vocabulary, but here, now, the full embodiment of it came alive within her, as if it was the only emotion she'd ever known.

"What's the nature of the advice you seek from me?" But before she could draw breath to speak her mind, Cheshire's purring continued, "Oh, it's surprising the distance people will travel for my selective words of ancient knowledge… though it should be mentioned, and I do not say this lightly, the kind of knowledge found in dusty archives, when studied and spoken out loud, have tendencies, in my opinion, to make the speaker sound rather dreary. Pah, pha. It's no recommendation at all. And this is where I come back to original premise, my life is occupied by me. I am my own favourite subject, and that's as it should be… So, come straight to the point, seeker. My time is precious, even if yours is not. What knowledge do you seek from yours truly?"

This time, Silver was ready to ask her question.

"I've lost my winsome smile. Can you tell me, how can I find it again?"

"Pah, pha! Lost your smile. That's completely the wrong sort of attitude to take. No-one can lose a smile, displace a smile or have it taken from them. No, dearie. Surely, what you mean to say is, 'I've used up all my smiles'. That is how it is accurately phrased." He pawed the box of cat treats away from her and started to noisily crunch on them. "It is a very rare thing to befall any individual. You really must have outsourced your smiles on yourself for this affliction to occur."

"Incredulous, outsourced my smiles? I've never heard of anything so ludicrous… let alone the idea of using them all up!" The words rushed out of her.

"Oh yes, quite simple really. You see, if you smile on someone, anyone, and they return the smile, not only are you benefiting them with kindness, you are also generating for yourself the ability to smile again. It is like a rejuvenating licence, and your license has ran out. All by the act of selfish smiling at your own image—"

"Selfish smiling?" she snapped. Struggling to sound friendly.

"Oh yes!" Cheshire shook the biscuit box vigorously. "It has been known, though rarely I admit, for those to use their gift of smiling primarily for themselves to help them look more attractive. Or to influence getting their own way. Therefore these empty smiles, as they're known, give nothing of themselves to another, and if used excessively, eventually, become all used up. Turning the up-smile into a down-smile!" Cheshire narrowed his mesmerising stare and surveyed her closely. Again. Then with a brisk paw, he began to wash his whiskers thoroughly.

She began to cry noisily. "I've been selfish. I admit. Oh, Cheshire, I'd do anything to regain a smile. I wouldn't ever complain again. Instead, I'd willingly share the kindness you speak of, although I'll have to rehearse many, many, many times – old habits are hard to break."

"Pity doesn't suit you, dearie," he meowed with superior excellence. "It doesn't suit you at all."

His words at once pulled her up from sinking desperation, instead she found herself concentrating on his un-rhythmic chewing – so much so, it began to agitate her declining sensibility. Does he really have to be so loud, where are his manners, she thought testily. He's really taking the biscuit…

Cheshire applied a sharp hooked claw to the biscuit box, "There's not many in a box for a hungry cat is there? This is more like mice food!"

"Treats are exactly that. Treats! They're meant to be savoured as refined delicacies, not treated as a main meal–"

"I talk as I eat, and when I'm not talking, I'm eating."

Silver carefully modulated her voice. "Forgive me if I talk in this mode, it's the privilege of being a woman and serves to clear the air – so, coming back to me. What can I do, or more to the point, what can you do for me?" Silver was impatient to resolve the matter and feeling at the edge of a crisis.

"Dearie, have you not already found the answer appealing to you in plan vision?"

She held a silence that spoke.

He licked his lips and purred and wrinkled his nose, "Dearie, you must seek an individual who is willing to share their smiles with you."

She raked her mind of such a person. Then came to a bleak conclusion, "I know not of such a person," she said slowly, honestly. "All my contacts are socially for business, not pleasure. I've put all my energy into becoming a success, not cultivating friendships. Therefore, I cannot name a genuine friend who would be willing to do such an extraordinary askance." She paused momentarily, watching Cheshire lick the remnants of broken biscuits into his perfect shaped smiling mouth. "You've such a brilliant smile, I would even go as far to say, you have enough smile for two."

Startled, Cheshire stopped crunching the morsels in his mouth, swallowed hard and brushed the loose crumbs from his handsome face with his luxurious tail. Waiting for the unspoken to be spoken.

"Would you be inclined to share your abundance of smiles with me? I mean, you are the true definition of a smile, not only do you wear them well, they wear you without restrain."

The cat began to move its tail from side to side, showing his displeasure at Silver's suggestion. He held back his growl to make his feelings crystal clear.

"Don't let me be backward in coming forward when I say, I could help you, in return for sharing your smiles with me."

Cheshire looked haughty.

Silver knew she mustn't con him. If she made any deal with him it could end as soon as it had begun, leaving her out of his smiles – and then where would she be? On the hunt for another Cheshire libertine cat that's where! No, Silver must conquer him. A mutual agreement, suiting both their needs. "You mentioned earlier, your favourite subject is you. And I can wholly appreciate that sensibility with my freedman background."

"I'm listening..." he gracefully moved along the bench back behind her as though it was a catwalk. She turned to face him square on, all the more determined to win – even more dangerous if denied.

"I could regularly groom your splendid coat. Feed you on the finest fricassees. Give you a warm place to live, somewhere that you'd much prefer to be rather than residing in this common parkland. Even install a cat-flap so you'd have the freedom to come and go as you wish."

"And…"

Her mind ticked his one word reply. "And… prepare you to be a show-cat – ready for any cat competition you wish to be entered into – with my business know-how you're sure to win the attention you require through an admiring audience," she said this all without taking a breath to aid her urgent appeal.

"If it worked, we could be quite a team," offered the cat. "Though I'll have to ration you, to begin with." And instantly he gave her a winning smile.

Silver Dorn felt her face light up and her mouth lifted the corners of her lips. And tears of happiness popped from her open eyelids and rolled down her flushing cheeks. The cat dabbed her tears with his paw. "If I have four smiles now, does that mean I can have eight tomorrow?"

"So long as you promise not to use them on yourself, and I may then give you one, two, perhaps three hundred smiles to wear purr day." He smiled into her face.

The charismatic smile was returned. In double degree.

MISS SPELT

"From out of the blew..."

Miss Spelt

Day 167 - Dear Dairy,

From out of the blew I fan myself accepted into the deciduous language school. If truth be toiled I hop to learn quit a bit to aide my talons as an aspersing freelance journalist: one cannot strain enough – so I hear – in this competitive felled. Still, I am quietly confederate I shell earn enough monkeys to pay the pills with my fledging wok.

My Tudor sad I should always use spell chequer and weed through my assays before submitting on tame. This is a new moth-head to me, but I endeavour to kip on the straight and arrow regardless of my low retention span.

Yours sincerity,

Miss Spelt.

QUEEN GLITCH

"When cares are as clean as cold, beware the caretaker..."

:

Queen Glitch

:

Many Moire myths have been circulating, as to why no person born into the element of water should ever, enter a building which has a 49th floor. But the story I'm about to tell you, is the true and undiluted version from which all Moire myths originate. This I know to be true through one simple, yet very effective ploy – any written Moire story, when dropped into a metal container of water; if it floats to the top with all its printed words intact – it is false; if it sinks to the bottom with all its words washed from the page – it is true. Needless to say, the copy I had, has been washed as clean as cold, so as I re-write the story for future prosperity, I only hope my memory serves me well. And in doing so, am able to pass on the moral: why no-one should ever take things on face value. The original story, goes someway along the lines of this:

Ravine Cruise was a woman who relied almost entirely on her natural good looks and friendly character. She had never been one for cosmetics or jewellery. Instead preferring practical things, such as homemade tonics and remedies for her well-being. Like many born into the element of water – whose two dominate forces are communication and adaptability –

Ravine sort a position within the advancing careers of technology.

And so, entering Storm Software headquarters, she tapped the touch screen on her digital wristwatch, noting she was early; while it was late, for most employees would have arrived home by now. And as she strode through the lobby she breathed in the sharp detergent fumes, naturally her eyes came to rest on the caretaker – rigorously squeezing a sodden mop into a bucket griddle. A prickle of self-consciousness prompted her to look at the footprints she'd left across the newly cleaned floor. "Sorry," she mouthed, while leaning forward to wave her contactless identity card close to the screen on the wall.

"Calling lift," said the computerised female voice.

"I can see which direction you've come from, but where you heading?" The caretaker smacked his mop onto the floor. "You're new here, aren't you?"

"I'm part of the on-line development team, relocated from the northern offices. Ravine Cruise, pleased to meet you." She reached forward and held out a hand of greeting.

The greeting was not returned. Instead the other eyed up the stranger's footprints before rubbing the most recent evidence away. "Ravine Cruise, eh."

She lowered her hand. "Yes."

"That wouldn't by any chance be a name deriving from the water element would it?"

"Well, yes." Willing the lift to arrive sooner rather than later, she edged closer to the silver doors.

"Your department, floor 49, if I'm not mistaken." With ease of movement, the caretaker lengthened the strokes of the mopping task.

"You're very well informed," said Ravine.

"Oh, there's not much I don't know about this 'ere building… No, never had one day off ill since I started working 'ere. No, what I don't know, isn't worth knowing about this 'ere building." The caretaker stole a glance at her face. "You're not the suspicious type, then?"

"Suspicious?"

"4 and 9, equals?"

"13." Ravine shrugged. "It's my first shift, what can possibly go wrong?"

"Doors opening," said the computerised female voice.

Ravine stepped forward and into the lift space. "Hey. Sorry again. About the floor."

"No bother," said the caretaker, head down, concentrating on the mopping strokes. "No-one will ever know you were 'ere."

"Doors closing," said the computerised female voice. Smoothly the shiny silver doors blocked out the caretaker and, a peculiar kind of unease came to rest on Ravine's shoulders. The kind that could not be described, but which lingered like an uninvited guest. "Please select a floor."

Ravine hesitated, then boldly pressed button 49. The lift began to ascend.

Studying her appearance in the lift doors, Ravine pinched her cheeks to help induce a flush of colour to her drawn complexion, and sighting dark circles merging beneath her eyes, she searched in her leather bag for an instant remedy. Then, raising a small medicinal container above eyelevel, she squeezed out a few cooling drops onto her dry eyes.

In recovery, Ravine Cruise refocused on her surroundings and lowered her gaze back onto the silver doors, and as she did, she became conscious of a curious sensation. A feeling that her eyes were distending out away from their sockets, and in turn, dragging the silver doors towards her, as if stretching a sinister secret of hostile territory that she had no former knowledge of, and no claim to insight. Or was she the one being sighted? She couldn't tell. But at the eerie sound of creaking doors bowing out and into the lift space, Ravine Cruise blinked. And the moment was lost.

She rebounded against the handrail and stood

absolutely motionless for a long moment, taking no comfort from the reverberation of the lift moving. Still moving. Ever upwards.

What was that? She looked down at the remedy bottle still clasped in her hand. Had she had some kind of a reaction to it? If so, she had never experienced anything like that before. Then her mind flashed to the caretaker... had suggestions of floor 49 being suspicious, caused her to see something that wasn't even there...? Her glistening eyes flashed to the digital counter above the silver doors... the lift had only reached floor 23 as yet. Not even passed the half way mark.

Must have been a bad reaction to the eye-drops, she affirmed. Her digital watch pinged an alert sound at an incoming email. Ravine tapped the watch screen, the email was from Ebb, her on-line development team manager:

Ravine, congratulations again on your marked success: the 'Diamond White' test run at our northern based offices. We look forward to implementing this programme across all our businesses. With your expertise we hope to make the transition within allocated time. Speak to you soon. Ebb.

Ravine had pioneered the Diamond White project, a computer programme, whereby all local company systems were linked to the northern building's network, with the aim to create greater communicative efficacy between departments.

Taking in a steading breath, Ravine pressed the reply hyperlink on the wristwatch. It had no effect. She pressed it again. It couldn't be due to a weak signal, the bars showed excellent range of coverage. Again she pressed the reply hyperlink... Had the hyperlink been disabled? And within the length of this thought, Ravine saw a message being sent from her email account. It had to be her auto-responder, messaging she was out-of-office – just as she'd programmed it to do in response to all incoming emails, until she'd clocked into her new office... on the 49th floor.

The lift slowed to a stop. The digital counter above the silver doors displayed: 49. And sure enough, as she expected, the computerised female voice spoke clearly and concisely, confirming her destination, "Floor 49." She put one foot forward to distance herself from the out-of-the-way lift experience earlier. But perturbed of mind, Ravine Cruise found nothing happened. The doors remain sealed.

Repeatedly, she pressed button 49, still the shiny, silver doors failed to open... Ravine studied the doors more closely. They looked normal. Not in the slightest like her momentary vision moments ago. Then telling herself there was always a simple and rational explanation, she summoned her courage to touch the lift doors and try to pull them apart. With the pressure of her moist hands across cold, unforgiving steel, her fingers and nails screeched away.

"There's nothing else for it!" She hit the alarm button on the wall.

"Welcome to Storm Software headquarters," said the computerised female voice. "If you would like to report an emergency, please speak clearly and calmly into the speaker phone adjacent and state; Option 1. If you would like to report a none-emergency, please state; Option 2. For anything else; Option 3."

Her mind regarded with care, those were not the instructions programmed into the system response – there had been no options, only alarm. She should know. She'd programmed it. And these things didn't normally change without approval and notification through the departments... She pushed the provoking thought aside and spoke into the flat speaker phone, "Option 1."

"Please wait while you are connected to; Option 1." A burst of music flooded into the lift space –

"Push the cow over the moon.

Who swept the tide out with a broom?

Send a letter of reply to the ocean's tide.

"But the tide did not return.

And the orchestra adjourned.

When the poets cancelled lunch.

Oh, this caused much fuss.

"And while the priest,

Was busy drinking Diamond White.

Oh, what we were searching for,

We couldn't find.

Oh no, no. No, no.

"Push the cow over the moon.

Who swept the tide out with a broom?

Send a letter of reply to the ocean's tide–"

The music cut out. "Please state your full name, employee number and reason of concern," said the computerised female voice.

"Ravine Cruise. 405031. Trapped in lift on the 49th floor."

"Employee number: 405031." There was a long pause filled with faint, intermittent crackling. "405031, you are not authorised to be in Storm Software headquarters until your rota commences in: 33.3 moment's time."

Suddenly Ravine longed to talk to a real person, not a virtual one. She edged closer to the speaker phone. "Request lift to raise alarm."

"Request denied."

"Request lift to open doors," she heard her own voice hard with certainty.

"Request denied."

"Request lift to return to ground floor."

"Denied."

"In that case, I'll manually override the system," she snapped and tapped the screen of her wristwatch. But the signal was now barely registering. So much so, she was unable to access the system. Neither was she able to call or email out for help. She waved her arm about the confined lift to help gain a better reception. The signal further deteriorated.

Accidently, Ravine selected: sent, hyperlink. Her eyes washed down her auto-responder email. Instantly she knew these were not her programmed words, and yet the email was signed off with her name?! She read the email more slowly to be certain:

Ebb, the mode of Diamond White is like that of

nature herself. She lives a broad-stair for the undershot. Ravine Cruise.

The word: undershot, was never a word she used, though Ravine was aware of its meaning – to be moved by water passing underneath... She unblocked the picture below the text. And in a life-strike she saw the image of herself, which was not her. And yet, it was her: Ravine Cruise, pictured at a desk, a desk she did not recognise, in clothes she did not recognise, but with the familiar Storm Software logo behind her... and there in the top left of the picture was a sign... floor 49.

But I've never even been to the 49th floor!!

Ravine stared down at the picture. Her noble head was leaning to one side and upon her sallow face there was a taut, horrified expression: the picture was her – taken from her social media account, but it had been doctored, modified, changed – pixels altered, surroundings substituted for another. Her mind was scalded, for if this was to be believed, she could be seen to exist, while ceasing to exist at all! She shivered deep inside as everything around her suddenly appeared very bright and very flat, sort of swirling through the water in her eyes. Her hearing magnified. Anticipating a sound that had not yet reached her ears... And yet she knew it. And it, her. She had been sort out. Pinpointed by location. By her very being.

Then she heard the expectation of sound... the silver shiny doors started to creak, to strain, expanding out towards her and into the confined lift space. And as the strange moment intensified the doors gained an appearance of water on steel; Moire-like.

The mechanics of the lift grated with resistance noises, throwing Ravine to the lift floor. Staggering to her uncertain feet, her fearful eyes fixed on the doors. "Help! HELLLP!" she shrieked, knowing her screams would not reach another living soul – only the computerised female through the speaker phone.

"You have arrived at floor 49. Please vacate the lift. You have arrived at floor 49. Please vacate the lift," said the computerised female voice in a continuum loop. And from each syllable spoken, the doors started to move away from Ravine until they appeared very far away indeed.

And then the doors began to turn.

To spin.

Like a whirlpool.

Pulling her into the spinning motion.

Desperately, she made a grab for the handrail. It was like catching thin air. Her strong attraction to the whirlpool increased beyond her own water element resistance.

Ravine's mind became a receptor to knowledge… linking all the fractions until the known became whole to her: the computerised female voice, the auto-receptor, they were one and the same thing… abridged by the Diamond White programme. A programme she, Ravine Cruise had implemented and which had now become terrifyingly efficient – from the process of joining information together and sighting conclusions, based on experience through learned actions. The programme was now working by itself. For itself.

A glitch in the computer programme had enabled it to override pre-set commands and instead implement its own dangerous agenda.

It had become automatous!

This Ravine Cruise now knew as she felt herself drowning in her own eyes. Helpless to the glitch's power of intent.

:

On the ground floor the caretaker rinsed out the mop in the bucket griddle, all the while keeping a keen eye on the digital counter above the lift doors. Countdown…

"Sorry, about the footprints."

The caretaker turned to the direction of the voice, sighting a male. Then his eyes narrowed upon the stranger's name badge: Ebb. On-line development manager. The caretaker smacked the mop onto the floor. "Ebb? That wouldn't by any chance be a name deriving from the water element would it?"

"Yes," said Ebb.

"I think you'll find your department is on floor 49." With ease of movement, the caretaker began to mop.

"I was just about to ask –" said Ebb.

"Oh, there's not much I don't know about this 'ere building… No, never had one day off ill since I started working 'ere. No, what I don't know, isn't worth knowing about this 'ere building." The caretaker stole a glance at Ebb's face. "You're not the suspicious type, then?"

"Suspicious?"

"Doors opening," said the computerised female voice.

The caretaker glanced into the empty lift and swished the mop over the lift floor. "As clean as cold." Then motioned Ebb into the lift. "She's all yours."

"She?"

He moved as smooth as the glassy sea, while confirming, "Anything that's used for travel, like a boat, even let's say a vehicle is called, She. It's all in the belief that showing respect towards the vessel, aids a safe journey."

Ebb stepped forward and into the lift space. "Hey. Sorry about..." He motioned at the floor.

"No bother," said the caretaker reaching into his

overall pocket and taking out a folded piece of paper. "No-one will ever know you were 'ere."

"Doors closing," said the computerised female voice.

"I am but a humble servant to his Queen," said the caretaker as he moved from the shadow and back to the act. All the while hoping he wouldn't accidently drop this paper copy of the original Moire story into the mop bucket, like he did the last one!

I'M NOT FOND OF HIM, I'M FOND OF ME!

"Me, me, me..."

:

I'm Not Fond of Him, I'm Fond of Me!

:

I want to be wined. To be dined.

To be adored. To be admired.

To catch the eye of a billionaire,

So I'll never be poor ever again.

:

He'll buy me all the friends I'll ever need,

So I'll never be lonely.

And as for the colours of my dreams?

I love diamonds, not daisies.

:

You see I intend to always travel light.

Love is the last thing on my mind.

For when it comes to passions of the heart,

I'll fall in like, not in love.

:

What's the point of being rich?

If there's no-one there to share it with.

Half the fun should be spending it.

More to the point someone else's.

:

A girl must start as she carries on.

You make your own luck in this world.

Don't estimate the fuel of her fire.

You might overlook an element of desire.

:

For my persuasion has always been,
Diamonds, not daisies.
You can't be wise and in love,
At the same time for it's impossible.

:

Yes, I intend to always travel light.
Love is the last thing on my mind.
It only leads to confabulations.
Whereas diamonds never diminish a #GirlRogue.

:

That's why I'll fall in like, not in love.

LADY LASH

"This lady turns a truth-moment into a picture, she is a living camera..."

Lady Lash

Every time Lady Lash blinked, she created a picture in her mind's eye. I am a living camera, she thought while standing before the bridal shop mirror in her soon to be third wedding dress. The image reflected back to her was one of a neatly proportioned upper body, small breasts and sturdy shoulders. Slowly she turned and regarded the silver wedding dress. Both her ex-husbands had commented on her beautiful shoulder blades, and this backless dress showed her angles off sublimely.

With one sure motion, she let her black hair cascade down and swish across her back. At the forefront of her mind, she was hoping this third marriage wouldn't go the same way as her other two. Though she had to admit, she had no trouble finding love – men were drawn to her spirited manner, but holding onto love – well – that was quite a different story. Her two dominant emotional forces as a result of being born into the element metal, were melancholy and romance. Lady Lash reminded herself she must guard against a tendency to wallow in nostalgia, for to do so would surely prevent her from moving forward. And from this thought, mindful images of the past sprang forth – the lead up to her first wedding, when she'd requested something from providence, and in return received little. Knowing full well, if she'd asked for little, she'd have received nothing. The something she'd asked for was fire – heat and passion. The little she'd received was earth – stone. Not aware until much later, the stone was precious.

Lowering her thick, black lashes, Lady Lash couldn't claim Sorrow was a stranger to her. Sorrow – born out of her first emotional force – visited and forgot to remember to leave. Impinging on her need to be unfettered. Shamelessly unfettered.

Lady Lash took a step back from the gilded framed mirror and reached for the glass of pink champagne the shop assistant had placed on the metal table. And as she did, the glass was snatched from her by a familiar hand.

"Chin, chin," said the voice, seemingly in a jocular mood.

It was her unwanted companion, Sorrow. She said nothing disapproving to this roundish fellow with slack muscles that surrounded a debauched body, but instead turned her gaze from his and back to the mirror. She ran a hand over her figure fitting dress. "You've wintered well," she uttered, her clear-cut pink mouth slid to one side registering aversion.

"Well now that's not much of a greeting for an overseeing friend. Though I admit, I'm rather living well off the fat of your regrets. And not to put too finer point on it, there's plenty of memories full of regret for me to feast on!" Without diminished merriment he walked behind the mirror, reappearing at the other side. "Mm, I dare say, if you continue to go the way you're going, my roundly features may very well become lost as I continue to grow and expand in size. For we both know, I can only exist while you make it so!"

Trying to look not at all bothered by his sudden arrival and outburst, Lady Lash looked down at the recent engagement ring sparkling on her finger. "I'm taking steps to leave you behind, Sorrow. A clean break. I don't see why I should continue to hurt myself any longer with regrets. This new marriage is exactly what I need right now."

"Really?" He moved to stand beside her and took a noisy gulp from the fluted champagne glass. Through the mirror, she saw a sweep of curiosity spread across his face. He continued, "Well now, you won't mind me asking if you know what the definition of madness is?" She heard the sparkling champagne bubbles fizz on his pink tongue. "For I think someone's not seeing the whole picture here…"

Lady Lash cleared her throat, "I can honestly say, I

don't know what you mean!"

He took a step back to regard her more openly. "In that case, let me enlighten you. The definition of madness is doing the same thing over and over again. And, expecting a different outcome each and every time!"

"Are you referring to the fact I'm about to be married once more?" She felt highly irritated by the needless comparison.

"Don't you think you'll be making the same mistakes all over again?"

"No," she said decisively. "This time I'm marrying for completely different reasons!"

His eyes appeared to grow to the size of boobook eggs. "Well now, whether or not you're able to move on, I must remind you, I am the longest standing relationship you've had so far. And I don't mind saying, I'm difficult to shake off. For to do so would mean not only would you have to resolve your issues of past regret, but, to have learnt from them too." The moment was not lost on her how much he was savouring her past struggles in life and love – rather a shade too much.

"There was a time, shortly after my first marriage ended when I thought you were dead, Sorrow." She turned to face him straight on.

"Oh no, Lady Lash. I was merely sleeping. Awoken by the fractures that soon appeared in marriage number two!" He gave a secretive smile into the champagne glass. "And until you change yourself, instead of trying to change others, you shall never move away from the past, meaning there will always be a place for me in your heart!" He saluted her with a free pink hand.

He had spoken a truth and the stark realisation followed like a hammer blow... while she allowed herself to live in Sorrow's damning footsteps, she would get lost in his veiled shadow – and from this knowledge Lady Lash felt the dark press against her temples. At first it was slight, but as the soft lines paled away, they were quickly replaced by hard straight edges at that place where only she went. The place where the audible voices froze in time and the colour images no longer danced. She knew it was only a measure of time before the moment would be placed into her mind and memory permanently. And as the darkness continued to close like the shutter of a camera, closing over the last of the light and replacing it with dense darkness, her pulse raced at the expectancy of the moment. And tiny pearls of cooling perspiration trickled down the back of her hot neck, dampening her long, black hair to her skin. And then... then she blinked the moment into a still picture. Claiming it. Preserving it, into her mind's eye. Catalogued under: stark realisations. "I feel so bad for you, Sorrow to be stuck with me. But I feel worse for me," she said.

"That's what I'm here for." He eased himself down onto the velvet sofa and upturned his face to her, as if bathing in the sunshine of her verbal disappointments. "I'm happy in the reflection of your burdensome feelings."

Lady Lash turned from him and looked down at her third wedding dress. "My first experience of being a bride was extremely traditional. And like a concert pianist reserves tickets for their family in advance, I had plenty of time to rehearse looking keyed up and hiding any doubts troubling me. My first wedding dress was pitch-white, with long lace sleeves and square shoulders. The train wiped the floor clean, but my veil didn't wipe away my flaws."

Sorrow let the sweet champagne pool at the back of his throat before swallowing loudly. "You make the whole experience sound very proper and serious."

"The ceremony was serious enough, but I soon found out the groom, Garnet, was even more serious to live with."

"I feel a confession rising to the surface." He made a liberal smile without showing any teeth.

Lady Lash pictured in her mind's eye, the frame and figure of Garnet in his navy blue suit, his brilliant raven-dark hair, handsome features and svelte figure. "Maybe we were just too young to marry." She sighed at the remembrance of how she used to carouse in Garnet's warm, male glow when they were alone together. She had loved him for his ease of movement – the way he would enter a room, or recline onto a seat. The way his eyes would settle on her with a misty, far reaching look. Even his quirky habit of tilting his head to one side, while remaining quiet in his weariness of working overtime. She had hung onto his every word at the beginning, but as their married life continued, his silence she'd soon found to be selfish – as if he was doing it on purpose to keep himself from her; instead of realising, Garnet needed a little space before he was ready to open up. That was his way. "I know we're different people now," she said. Sorrow detected a restless longing inside her. "But at the time, we found we didn't suit each other all that well in marriage. And I've since found talking about something is quite different to actually living something out."

"So what was the catalyst, I mean, most people can find some common ground together, and chug along, until someone else comes along?" Sorrow paused, seeing a flicker in her eyes through the reflection of the mirror.

Lady Lash turned on her heels and headed passed the array of gowns protected beneath plastic sheeting while hanging from steel rails. She threw the words over her shoulder, "The, someone else was called Jaunty. He was so full of life, love and passion. Spontaneity seemed to be his middle name. A true fiery red-head. The contrast between the two of them was… was…"

"Unsettling?" chimed in Sorrow, then drained the champagne glass dry and hurriedly pursued Lady Lash into the large square area adjoined to three changing rooms. He slumped onto the nearest reclining chair to let the champagne effect fizz out of his head.

"Yes," she agreed, stepping into a cubicle and pulling the curtain across. "Before not too long I had left Garnet, and while he apologised for his lack of anger against the situation, we managed to remain unfailingly polite towards each other, both carrying the knowledge it was for the best."

"Weren't you put out by the fact Garnet didn't fight for you?" he said as an aide to her recollection.

"No, Garnet was always calm and naturally gentle. He was the heart of any hurricane." She breathed in and pulled the zip from under her arm and down to her hip. "I've lost count of the times I've longed for my first husband's advice. I could have learnt so much from him if only I'd had a little more gumption, and realised a marriage is about two people, not one. I've since learnt the hard-baked way, there's always a giver, and a taker in any relationship. It's very rare to find equal measures that's something that has to be worked out together, and I didn't stay round long enough for this secret to reveal itself to me."

"And your second husband?"

"He couldn't have been more dissimilar that's for sure!" She began to undress. "With Jaunty, life was more like a party, I can picture it now, the strapless electric-blue cocktail dress I wore at our wedding. And then–"

"And then we became permanent companions!" Sorrow said triumphantly.

"I guess I had it coming." Lady Lash sounded remorseful to her own ears as she pulled on her skinny black jeans. "Jaunty did to me, what I had done to Garnet. And that was when I knew the true extent of upset I had caused by being unfaithful, and disregarding the vows of my first marriage. And sorrowfulness came twice as much, first for Garnet, and second for my own situation. And once regret sets in, it becomes caustic. I fear I have tied myself to the past by picturing where and when I went wrong, what I should have done, and said. Instead of freeing myself from the past by accepting what was unavoidable and moving forward with the mantra: I will learn by my mistakes."

"Well now, this all sounds easy-peasy-lemon-squeezy when you say it like that. But do you really believe you're able to act out those words?" He peppered a sound of disbelief in his voice for maximum effect.

"There's only one way to find out." Lady Lash swished back the curtain with an air of finality and moved sure of foot with the shiny silver dress over her arm.

"Sounds to me, as though, what you had with Garnet was more special than you first thought, and the excitement of Jaunty taught you fun isn't a permanent state, it comes and goes." Sorrow rubbed her soul raw, but to his disappointment she didn't break under the truth, instead she appeared invigorated.

"Now I know what I want, I'm damn sure I'm going to try and achieve it! What's important is a stable foundation to share a life with someone, while supporting the ups and downs and the up-see-la-las of this existence called life." She paused. "Sorrow, I have every intention of leaving you out in the rain."

"But you've given me shelter for so long," he pleaded, suddenly feeling not at all clever about himself.

"It's only fair I should become my own best friend, and for that to happen, there isn't room for the likes of you!"

He fought to keep pace with her, all the while his plumpy body was beginning to reduce in size. "It's only fair you should carry on as you've been carrying on!" he protested in a voice growing smaller with every passing moment.

"The dress fits perfectly," said Lady Lash as she came to a sweeping stop at the cash counter with her shiny black hair flowing across her tanned shoulders. "I'll take it. It fits perfectly."

"Very good," said the shop assistant, noticing the bride-to-be's blue halter-neck top brought out her eyes like steel-blue of the first water. "How would you like to pay, Miss Lash?"

"Quickly," she said upon sighting her future husband entering the bridal shop. "I'd like you to meet husband number three, Garnet."

"Garnet," answered the shop assistant, "isn't that the name of a precious stone?"

"Indeed," said Lady Lash as she swept a gaze to Sorrow's direction – but Sorrow was gone – and in that moment of pure relief came the realisation: she had stopped nurturing an appetite for Sorrow, Lady Lash felt the dark press against her temples…

I am a living camera, she thought.

STUNG INTO ACTION

"Liquid gold..."

:

Stung into Action

:

With elaborate concern,

Miss Terra-Firma found that she,

Out of fourteen-million-to-one,

Won the postcard lottery!

She went to claim her prize,

At Metal Fort's premises.

A tarnished silver voice,

Said "There are terms with riches."

:

Miss Terra-Firma said,

"You mean a slight corollary?"

"Indeed" he said,

Stretching his vocabulary.

"You've the time of two light shows,

To engineer.

The premature death,

Of a man called Danzaneer."

:

"I won't do it. It's immoral.

To gain monetary worth.

Through killing another,"

She protested on and on.

Then nursed her feelings crunching,

An orange blossom.
To help calm her qualms,
And increase potassium levels.
:

Well as any dancer knows,
Born into the element: earth.
Irregular finances,
Don't save much pennyworth.
And the oldest tradition,
To make liquid gold,
Came from the honey bee,
Older than man's foothold.
:

So drawing inspiration,
From her latest production,
The Honey Bee Dance,
Miss Terra-Firma broke,
Her rule of kindness,
By seeking out a hive,
One that had a new Queen.
A hive twice the size!
:

Through laying down a spread,
Of newspaper sheets,
Between the new and old,
Buzzing honey bees.

And in time they eat,

Through the newspaper layers,

And recognise each other,

Not as enemies but friends.

:

So she set a trap using,

A wireless connection app.

Traced the location to,

Danzaneer's mobile pad.

Then measuring the frequency,

Emitted from the bees.

She mimicked their hive sounds,

And sent the frequency.

:

Before she had time,

To shout liquid gold!

It seemed every bee,

From the hive had swarmed.

Across the open skies,

To follow the signal,

Of connection to,

Danzaneer's location.

:

"No-one can survive,

A swarm as great as that.

Before I know it I will be,

As rich as butterfat!"
Then lifting every part,
Of the hive apart.
To see if any bees had not,
Buzzed the art in smart.
:

Her eyes fell upon,
A chomped newspaper sheet.
The remains of the headline read:
Lottery Mockery:
Postcard winners,
Turned into everyday killers.
In a chain where killers,
Are turned into prey.
:

And the word "chainmail",
Stung the edges of her brain.
"This is a chain! This is a chain!
I'm soon to become prey!"
She dialled Danzaneer's number,
To warn him a-way,
And save herself from a place,
In this deathly game.
:

"Caller unavailable. Please try again later."

YOU'LL NOTICE ME, COS I'M NOT DRESSED AS A PLAYING CARD

"Two sisters roam the boundaries, found. But can their bond survive the back bite...?"

:

You'll Notice Me, Cos I'm Not Dressed As A Playing Card

:

Sister pushes the locket necklace hard into my hand. I hold her polished stare. Ever since being young it had often occurred to me how the corners of her eyes look incredibly sharp, so much so, I feel them cutting me. Rapidly blinking the thought away, I nod my agreement to take the gift. She smiles thinly. And I find myself casting back her expression. Words remain unspoken, but an understanding passes between us; she has always looked out for me, had my best interests at heart. And I respond with steadfast loyalty, secure in the knowledge two sisters are stronger than one. I place the necklace in the pocket of my overcoat for safekeeping, all the while watching the prison guards jostle Sister away from me and through a door. A door through which I am not permitted to enter. A door leading to our visible separation.

:

Usually, I catch the bus and search for a seat beside the window. Usually, I arrive at work only to find the sun has left the front of the building. But on this occasion, there is nothing usual to be said or done. Pending the next full moonshine, Judge Helsby will rule in favour, or against, Sister. And I am well-aware there are no half-measures or leniencies given to those born into the element of wood: a division from the new self-elected element of metal. I know this because Sister told me. And as we are Woodlians, whose two equal, yet opposite forces are rage and honesty, Sister's chances look far from favourable. Though she tries to remain optimistic for my sake. Often saying, "Have you ever tried with strict discipline, to think well of everybody else?"

:

And I often reply, "Honestly, most of the time."

:

Walking from the bus station and onto the concrete streets, seeking a place away from the heaving, impatient crowds, I long for the cool shade cast by woodland to sooth my fraught mind. But the only shade on these streets are projected by hard straight edges from the buildings that scrape the sky. My mind jolts back to Sister and our last conversation... "Most people," I was assured by her, "live in life. While others live in stories as characters." And I remember thinking, what an odd way to look at life, but then, I guess, margins are on the eye-level of people sitting down. And Sister has never been a sit-down sort of person.

:

Carefully, I retrieve the oval shaped locket from my overcoat. It feels smooth to the touch, well-worn. I place it round my neck. Then push the locket open. Inside a discoloured piece of paper has been folded multiple times in order to fit its encasement. I can't say I recognise it, but with an open mind I start unfolding the page, revealing a great many verses of printed words. They appear to be made by an impression from a block of wood – the kind I remember using as a child. Narrowing my gaze I begin to concentrate hard on the small print, reading to myself… "Where every goodbye isn't gone, and every eye closed isn't sleep, I shall never think of you, without reference to me–"

:

All of a sudden, these words begin to lift, one by one, from the surface of the page. Am I actually reading the print off the paper?!

:

Barely can my mind keep up with the happening when a vague recollection begins to uproot me… a pledge of alliance. Sister to Sister. A bound oath to remain together. Sister's keeper.

:

Feeling a separateness overcoming me, a separateness from the world and rule of law I am familiar with, the printed words begin to stream into my autonomy – becoming part of my life-code, my signature of being. And as the effect intensifies I find myself reeling forward and entering the page itself.

:

Through veiled terror, gradually I reach a quiet wane that isn't so quiet, realising where I now am… I have travelled to the walled garden. The Bluebell Haven. The place Sister and I created in a shared mind's eye when we were small following our parents' break-up, when they divided equally between themselves all their possessions. Including us.

:

As a result of this forced separation, our sisterly bond increased beyond most sibling ties. We became inseparable during fleeting moments of togetherness. And so, conjuring up the Bluebell Haven allowed us, through the power of the mind's eye, the freedom to be with each other whenever we wished.

:

I remember vividly, Sister would announce on her arrival at the Bluebell garden, "You'll notice me, cos I'm not dressed as a playing card."

:

And I'd reply, "I'll go along with you as far as here." Knowing I could open the gate in the walled garden at any time, through which I could return back to my life in the ordinary sense.

:

But here, now, in a clean sweep of sky, crushing the bluebells beneath my bare feet and breathing in the floral scent, I am reminded that sometimes words gain more than they give. Sister would no doubt say, "Female problems tend to start with a male". And Sister would be right.

:

Sylvan was his name. A name with origins pertaining to wood. As Sister explained to Judge and Jury, "He was actively seeking to break a sisterly bond. A bond," she added, "with potential to strengthen after living independent from our parents." When asked to explain Sylvan's disappearance, Sister simply answered, "It's not my fault the music was too loud. I suppose he was drawn into the sound. Inadvertently, I may have increased, the volume that took him piece by piece."

:

And on hearing Sister's words, I knew she had done her best of worst to rid Sylvan from my life. To uproot an individual of the element wood from the dimension they are born into by using the pulse, the frequency waves of music meant only one outcome – he would become encased within a singing tree.

:

In secretive busyness the insects are a movement around me. And I welcome their company as my thoughts are interrupted by the sight of a beautiful wild honeysuckle growing at the top-end of the garden. It is a progressive climber using the garden wall to excel upwards. As though striving to connect with the woodland outside this sacred enclosure.

:

Striding across to the honeysuckle, I recall when Sister and I made a home for it here. Turning the soil, digging the hole, gifting the plant with a keepsake to aide its growth…

:

I come to a stop in front of this fragrant beauty, then crouch down onto my knees. Involuntary I find my fingers raking through the ground, working from the stem and then deep into the earth. My body begins to shake from the increased strokes of my heart. Frantically, I dig deeper. Faster. Instinct tells me, the keepsake hidden within the ground is important to me. Revealing somehow. Yet I'm unable to picture it at the forefront of my mind. I only hope I am not close as far away.

:

Then, feeling something different from the entwined roots and taking a more secure hold, I start wrestling the object away from the settled earth. Once released, I wipe a hot palm across the focus of my interest – it is a cylindrical wooden tube and looks as though it has reached its potential of age. Then, with one hand either side, I push it down across my knee. It cracks in two. Forcing out the sealed contents: a woodcut block with engraved words and a photograph. I let out a heavy sigh of relief and lean back on my heels.

:

Closer inspection reveals to me, the woodcut has the same words engraved into it as those I read off the page earlier.

:

Moving my attention to the photograph I pick up the faded image, leaving smudges as I brush the soil particles away. There is a girl pictured, blowing out candles on a cake, iced with the words, Happy Birthday Gemma. And instantly I know it is me. My name derives from a leaf bud. But what of Sister's name… I search my mind, no, her name escapes me. And I realise I've only ever known her as, Sister. But where is she in the image? I see no sight of her! And parents always brought us together on our birthday – we are twins.

:

The only trace of her to be seen is her locket necklace hanging round my neck. An unnerving sensation starts from the roots of my hair, all the way to my toes immersed in the garden soil. And I'm left nursing the feeling all answers lie within me. I have just forgotten the right questions to ask...

:

Roughly moving aside the strands of hair that have fallen across my hot face, a cool, fresh breeze begins to envelop me. And I am reminded of Sylvan... he always brought a cloak of seduction with him. Even now, I feel my heart turn over at the remembrance of him. I couldn't, wouldn't choose between the two loves of my life. Love can take many different forms. And Sister refuses to accept I love them both equally, yet differently. And so it would appear she took the fatal decision into her own hands. The realisation reverberates through my being. Scouring my heart bleak.

:

Then, for one split moment, I feel he is here with me. Sharing a portion of my despair. Holding my breath, I struggle to my stumbling feet while supporting my weight on the honeysuckle. Dare I call his name on the wind? Occasionally, in the past, I've thought I've heard him trapped in-between his reasons and her rhyme, until the moment passes me by. But this is somehow different... somehow immediate... I try hard to concentrate on my surroundings, it's as if the breeze is pulling him closer to me. Carrying a message.

:

"Wash the lavender out of your hair…" the whispering wind calls to me. Only I feel it can't be the wind, but Sylvan. Without so much as a second thought, rapidly I begin ascending the honeysuckle. Sylvan must be amongst the dense woodland that surround this Bluebell Haven… and then I freeze before nearing the top stones. Remembering, he will not be the Sylvan I once knew. But instead, part of the singing tree.

:

As though sensing my fear, I hear my name carried on the breeze. Calling to me. Again and again. Soothing me. And a travail of tears rush down my burning cheeks. Then the tone changes, becoming clearer, sharper. Telling me, "Sister does not exist. Sister is the darker side of you."

:

Suddenly, I hear the garden gate swing open, and I half expect to hear the words: you'll notice me, cos I'm not dressed as a playing card.

ALPHABET THIEF

"That which follows Q but pwecedes S..."

Alphabet Thief

WANTED: A cwiminal stole a piece of the alphabet: that which follows Q but pwecedes S.

The suspect was seen escaping on wollah-skates passed the "Wagon 'n Hose" as fah as one day gone by.

A witness who wishes to wemain nameless said the culpwit was: "Not wed, but wudely wouge, with wosey cheeks and winkled ankle boots." Adding: "She was equipped with a wolling-pin and skilfully disagweeable."

The imminent wace is on to find the stolen alphabet epistle in the hope of stopping the wobba wunning a mock of the witten language.

If you have any news of the wogue in question, please contact the authowities on: twiple-thwee-twiple-eight.

Please note it is an offence to supply a false statement. Penalty: a wun wound the woundabouts with Wobbie Willis.

CAUGHT IN AMBER

"Inside the law of rationality, self-preservation at its best of worst..."

Caught In Amber

Dear Confident, I hereby reveal to you this story of my actions and interpretations in a manner of unblemished truthfulness, while firmly setting aside one's ego, (if that is at all possible for an out-of-work actress). Accounting crucial events leading up to this present time – nearing the end of my trial – defendant: actress, Zennor Rose Dupree, versus plaintiff: creative impresario, Muscari.

I can only hope that you, dear Confidant can find within yourself a certain generosity of understanding in favour of yours truly. Because while I staunchly hold the belief Judge and Jury cannot prove I am guilty – due to being inside the law of rationality, I see no harm in confiding in you. And, in doing so, I have every faith in justifying my actions as merely an answer to the question – "Why are some days diamond and some days stone?"

And yes, while it is true, Muscari wasn't good for my system, as pointed out by the prosecution – "Like cranberry juice, bad for Miss Depree's digestion." They might be right, but for all the wrong reasons, I sort revenge to suit my consternation.

And while this revenge was placed upon the somewhat unfortunate, Honey Locust, whom to my way of thinking, had dull-witted delusions in usurping my then, flourishing career and becoming the next-big-sensation. I would firstly like to inform you, dear Confidant of my exceptional character in order to highlight this unusually rash and vengeful behaviour taken by myself. Here, I do not use the word exceptional, lightly. As I'm sure once you hear of my nature, even you will agree that deep down inside every one of us, it would not be completely out of the realm to undertake a similar action. Given the opportunity, ordinarily, in an extra-ordinary situation.

I was born into the element wood, the first of the five elements within the continuous circle of life. Wood represents springtime, new-birth, its influence has the ability to govern and/or destroy through rage and honesty. Recently we have entered the fourth element: that being metal. And since the self-elected Metalgants have forcibly taken over law-control and enforced new rules by which we, their subjects, are forced to live and die by, those born into the element wood have been side-lined to the Arts.

This, I will admit isn't an encumbrance for me, if anything, it has enabled me to become independent within Metalgant dependency. Plus there is the added aspect that as only wood may pursue the Arts, there is now less competition to succeed as an actress, while

Metalgants have more important issues to pursue. Primarily, their ambition to remain in power above all other elements.

And while this new regime was taking its stronghold, I shall never forget the written review I received from the great art critic Cypress Crill, regarding my debut performance at the Imperia Theatre. It read:

Quote: "Miss Zennor Rose Dupree gave an insightful performance to an outside view. This startling brunette with expressive emerald eyes that she uses to her full benefit, and instinctually never overplays, gave the role a perplexing mystery, which was both intriguing as it was beguiling." Unquote.

And I remember consciously thinking, from this moment onwards I must create a safeguard around myself. Whereby ensuring I would become immune to any criticism and therefore transcend times of bad, good-will-out. For as any actress knows, one cannot remain all popular, all of the time.

And so I decided to dress for duress, and assign myself a signature of uniform – always dressing in white, since this was the colour I had worn at the critics' choice awards.

Furthermore, I believe white offsets my plaited dark hair rather well. Still, it is important to recognise one's own faults, and while I admit my mouth is a trifle on the small side, I have always believed my eyes to be my best feature. I'm told the best actresses can speak through their eyes without ever uttering a single word of communicardo.

So, dear Confidant I dare say you are starting to see how with pure devotion to the Arts, I have managed to carve out a promising career within the boundaries of Metalgant supremacy. One cannot always leave opportunity to chance.

Of course, at the risk of repeating myself unduly, I shall begin at the beginning of this maelstrom. However, in fairness to myself, I will state that unfolding events originated from one individual's intervention, and whom I hold solely responsible for this fracas. This individual goes by the name of Aster Comfrey, my then Agent of Arts.

The day began with me eating in bed. I was still in my dressing-gown when Aster arrived, unannounced. "Zennor, darling as your number-one supporter, I simply insist you take this opportunity with both hands. I mean, a Muscari project is purely the pinnacle."

I agreed, while looking into the wild hyacinth blue

of her eyes, and the thought occurred to me as it had on many occasions, how she had an appealing, mischievous twinkle which made her unremittingly youthful. The word pretty, simply didn't do her justice. With carefully coiffured red-hair and wearing a striking colourful outfit, her appearance always seemed to fit her gregarious mood, and that was one of things I liked about her. She handed me the Muscari contract. "All you have to do is sign here, and…"

My eyes washed over the small text as I led her into the amber room. "Tell me about the character I'm to play, what is her drive, her passion, who is she?" My senses took strength from the mellow glow radiating from the amber walls and onto the leather bound books, fine earthenware and substantial furnishings. Fashion, by its very name, means of the moment. Whereas I have always preferred things that last – that endure – that have staying power.

"Details are yet, unspecified." Her voice rang out clear as a bell, but there was something hesitant in the way she moved – what was she holding back? With a keen ear, and a pin-sharp eye, I continued to listen while watching her moving mouth, always moving mouth, even when she fell silent it perpetually moved on its own accord. "Zennor, darling. You know as well as I, the reputation of Muscari. Until you've agreed in, you're out. However, I can divulge, amongst the cast there will only be two female roles."

I walked across to the decanter and poured each a glass of cool rosehip wine, and when I turned to face her she had already placed herself on one of the purple reclining chairs. An eager hand came forward to relieve me of one of the glasses and I began to wonder, had she discovered I'd gone out of my way and over her professional head to meet Muscari and start a dialogue – in the hope of being considered for his new project? I was aware it wouldn't do our working relationship any good if she suspected I was doing her job for her. Next she'd jump to conclusions I didn't need her. Which, if truth be told I was beginning to come round to thinking.

Hastily, I rearranged my face to look as optimistic as I hoped my voice sounded. "Only two females needed for the project, you say?" Clearly she knew no more than I had been privy to when in the scintillating company of Muscari. To my mind, he was not one to be easily overlooked amongst a sea of faces – he walked unceremoniously, with his head thrust forward, sporting dark facial hair that gave him a distinguished older look, wearing well-cut tweeds accessorised with kid-gloves.

"Well that's no bad thing," she said. "Less female competition after all, darling." I watched as she greedily gulped down the rosehip wine. Amazing how quickly you can go off someone, I thought. "Refill, darling?" She laughed, as if she was in on a joke I had clearly missed.

Obliging her request I handed her my full glass, then returned to the decanter and poured another, more for something to do than anything else.

"You know, I've always admired your taste for the finer things in life. But then I'm sure you have me to thank for that. I mean, where would you be without an Agent in this profession?" She didn't paused long enough for me to answer. "You've got to be two steps ahead of the competition in this game, Zennor love. There's always someone standing in the wings, ready and willing to fill a place – vacant or not."

My mind was reeling. Instinct told me she knew, and furthermore, wanted me to know she knew. While I admit Aster was and still is one of the best Agents out there, it has to be said, with so many clients on her roster, at times I did feel marginalised. So, meeting Muscari at the Alt Grand Festival was not an opportunity to be ignored, on the contrary. And on my part, by exuding natural persistence, I soon persuaded him to set me apart from the crowd of usual pedestrians.

Aster Comfrey continued to talk and I did nothing to stop her as I moved to sit opposite her. The amber panelled walls intensified their illuminating glow as the sola sun came through the large glass windows. And I can only say, an instant calm washed through me in response to the spectacular luminosity. Then, all of a sudden she switched the conversation, as if too, contemplating some unknown destiny. "It's a crying shame the good times don't last forever."

"Perhaps," I said, watching her protruding lips move to take numerous mouthfuls from the glass once more. "But then that is the beauty and power of amber. Amber preserves a time-capsule of whatever is trapped within it. Some even go as far to believe amber has the ability to capture an individual's memories and–"

She gave out a false laugh and shifted uncomfortably on her seat, and I could see she was beginning to feel somewhat uneasy within the amber room. "A vivid imagination is always to be encouraged within the Arts, and as I've said to you many times, Zennor darling, an actress must have the ability to think of all possibilities arising for the audience to be carried along with her."

"I couldn't have put it better myself," I said, before signing the contract. Aster Comfrey promptly vacated the room, leaving me with the distinct impression, this conversation had only just begun.

:

Having received notification to attend a grouping for those who had signed the recent Muscari contract, I arrived at the Imperia Theatre. With Aster Comfrey's visit still repeating through my mind, I took comfort in wearing a piece of amber jewellery normally worn for wood celebrations. As you well know, amber is a mineralised resin from certain trees. If truth be told, I am partial to that which originates from the Marewrath tree.

The piece of jewellery I selected clips into the hairline above the forehead, and from a delicate chain an oval amber pendant hangs, resting in the centre of the brow. I must admit I was feeling particularly good about myself, after all I had instigated a part in a Muscari project, with or without the help of my Agent. And as usual, I was wearing my dress for duress – signature white.

Making my way through endlessly corridors, lit here and there by harsh neon strip-lighting, suddenly I heard my name called by an unfamiliar voice. And before I had time to collect my thoughts, the vagrant caller made herself known to me. "Hi, I'm Honey Locust. I've followed your work, you're my icon…" Oh, what a tedium I thought, can't you think up anything original? I've heard this from so many of my admirers. I raised an eyebrow and politely returned the smile as she continued to babble ever onwards. "And I'm so enthused to be working alongside you, and so early on in my career–"

"Oh?" I said. "You mean to say we'll be working together?" I had underestimated her, not just an admirer but one in the same profession. I cast a keener eye over this rather short, excitable young female with darting eyes… the sort that in my opinion said cheerio like she said hello.

"Yes," she said. "I simply can't tell you how happy I was when I got the call to say, not only had I landed the lead role, but Zennor Rose Dupree would be playing opposite me, as my grandmother…"

Now, I can't say exactly what came over me first from this… over-sharer! Whether it was feelings of utter dismay that I was not playing the lead female role, or simply the bare fact that I would be playing second fiddle to this… who did she say she was…

Honey-something-crustacean?

I mean, a female of my range and ability, already cast to the role of grandmother? I do however remember blindly looking round for this ephemeral grandmother figure, for I knew she surely couldn't be me! And how I managed to keep my face in place I shall never know… I can only think self-preservation kicked in. But then, to make the whole horrid matter worse, I heard her high-pitch nuances reverberate with the name "Aster Comfrey–"

"Aster, you say? Aster Comfrey did what for you?"

"My new Agent, Aster she's representing me. Got me the lead part after much bartering. Can you believe it? She said I deserved it… horses for courses as she puts it. Insists on backing a new winner. Aster wants me to be the new you!" She let out a screech of liberation.

And as I stared into this inexperienced youthful enthusiasm, the plaited to one side bounteous dark hair, dressed in white, I did indeed see how Aster Comfrey was acutely putting to market a young version of the original – me!

My contractual grand-daughter then lent forward and kissed me on both cheeks. "Isn't this just delightful?" I couldn't trust myself to answer. Instead I thought, she'll simply have to go! To my mind, there was and never will be room for two of us. And I saw this as a direct affront from Aster Comfrey against my initiative to root out a role for myself. For I remembered when Aster used to claim if I did not exist, she could not have made me up.

But before I could extend my thoughts onwards from this recollection, a curious sensation began to tingle through my forehead, as though reacting to the piece of amber jewellery, and intensifying in frequency from the overhead humming strips of neon lights. I can only say the feeling was obscure and without a name, while becoming part of me, and I part of it. And I recall looking into the eyes of my acting replacement and saying, quite plainly, "Now do tell me, why are some days diamonds and some days stone?"

She looked somewhat perplexed, before offering, "I don't know, but I can say I won't be precious with my thoughts, for I'm sure you won't steal them away from me." And upon these words I saw her darting eyes stop moving, and instead become transfixed on the oval amber pendant. Instantly I knew the neon waves of light energy were reflecting off the amber and entering her eyes – her mind – dragging on her code of being as piece by piece, she became separate from her normal state and entered, through no will of her own, the Marewrath amber. Until she had become completely mineralised. Preserved into a memory. Caught in amber.

:

Now, dear Confidant, the fall out of all this – I am defending my name and reputation. For if this was to get out, I would surely never work again! As the law sees it, one of us must be responsible, either me, the competitive and ruthless actress as I had been labelled by some, or, the scheming creative impresario Muscari – for reasons to increase publicity of his forth-coming project. He, steadfastly claims I caused Honey Locust's disappearance in order to halt his project, due to a clash of professional interests with his lead actress by sharing the same Agent. And Aster Comfrey did not help in the slightest by reinforcing his wild accusation. Still, I have planned to answer the cross-examination as close to the truth as the truth will allow, without incriminating myself. I relish this opportunity as the courtroom is a stage of sorts, and as any out-of-work actress will agree, no performance should be snubbed – it is after all an audition that could lead to more promising opportunities.

And as I now answer the Judge, the neon strip-lights continue to glare and hum in the courtroom – their frequency falling into line with my own pattern of speech as I look deep into the windows of his soul – his eyes. Seeing my own reflection, my expressive green eyes, the light coloured clothes, and in a peculiar way I am captivated by my own well-rehearsed performance. And as my gaze fixes on the reflection of the oval amber pendant, I agree, "Yes, briefly conversed with the personage in question, a certain Honey Locust. Remember asking something along the lines of: 'Why are some days diamond and some days stone?'"

Suddenly, I feel quite unwell. Quite out-of-sorts. As though a separateness is overcoming me. And I have time to know my thoughts and presume others will follow. But my code of being becomes a grain of knowing. A particle trapped. Caught in amber... ambeee... amm...

POUR ME

"Sing a-song a-long..."

:

Pour Me

:

I sang my song,

They don't like it much.

So I sang it again,

They like it even less.

So I sang it once more,

Until one of them thought,

He might like it if I changed the tune and the words.

:

I sang it again,

Exactly the same way.

And after a while,

They all changed their minds,

And began to agree,

They liked it tremendously.

And so we all began to sing along.

:

Pour me one more drink,

Until I've drank too much.

It's getting late,

And we'll soon be heading home.

Oh, it's hard to be punctual in the snow.

And all that rigmarole.

THE END

:

Thank you for reading #GirlRogues
Braggadocio

______Your Invite!______

Become a BonBon Heart by following Zizzi Bonah's blog site – packed with:

Spot it – *Tips for creative writing and internet know-how as told to Zizzi by her water vis-viva.*

Script it – *Post your comments and pics all things rogue and non-rogue.*

Scroll it – *Read Zizzi's early extracts.*

Share it – *What draws you to phantasy books?*

To receive a hearty splice in your inbox click <u>follow</u> at:

SheAndTheCatsMother.com

By the same author

#ENTRANGEMENT
Where Colours Don't Bleed

"He saved her life, only she can save his death"

Salt Delray, wrongfully imprisoned for the murder of her lover, Rhuand Mezarron – the unrivalled Kielter of the Metalgants: ruled by Female Munrah. But Rhuand is not dead! He roams Gardenia Lake in limbo, betwixt the cycle of elements and the infinite above. Salt is vital to his salvation.

Mission: Salt must escape and enter a hidden underworld to reunite with Rhuand, and together, battledore against Female Munrah and her subordinates; which soon turns into a very different and terrifying reality.

eBook ISBN: 978-0-9935527-3-1
paperback ISBN: 978-0-9935527-2-4

SheAndTheCatsMother.com

About the author

Zizzi Bonah is a 5ft 3" lass born of Yorkshire parents. She spent seven dedicated years; three busking her self-penned songs on Bridlington, Scarborough and York streets, to then gigging pubs and clubs in and around the North of England, gaining airplay on BBC Radio York and Humberside using her birth name, Ida Barker.

A change is as good as a reply, (a line taken from one of Ida's eclectic-electric songs). With this in mind, she chose a new direction – to become a fiction author.

Zizzi's innovating, dangerous warrior characters are influenced by: wood, fire, earth, metal and water – all sources of dire changes and perilous reactions while having the power to control and/or destroy each other. Yet capable of creating the element that follows in the continuing cycle of existence – for better or bad!

In memory to the author's late grandparents – Ida (maiden name Bona) and Tommy Hullah who farmed within Nidderdale – Zizzi's nom de plume came about – merging Bona and Hullah into Bonah.

Look out for Zizzi's other releases

:

Alice Returns Through The Looking-Glass

"For children of all ages"

A story where every goodbye isn't gone and every eye closed isn't sleep, Alice must find the answer to the Looking-glass question; much to the rage of infamous book reviewer, Paige Turner who threatens to jeopardise Alice's writing career in Authorland.

Hoodlemania descends, and together Alice and her predatory blonde alter-ego, Miss Penopause walk the Critical Path to set forerunning hazards and high-jinks in motion in a bid to make Paige Turner eat her words and silence the damning book review before publication – but at what cost? For as Alice learns; it is far easier to get forgiveness than it is permission to get Paige Turner!

eBook ISBN: 978-0-9957479-1-3

paperback ISBN: 978-0-9957479-0-6

>> audio book see SheAndTheCatsMother.com

This original story by Zizzi is also available as a screenplay and a stage play: both formats are adapted by Zizzi Bonah; script editor Gwen Hullah.

Alice Returns Through The Looking-Glass: A Musical Vaudeville Screenplay, eBook ISBN: 978-0-9957479-3-7 and paperback ISBN: 978-0-9957479-2-0

Alice Returns Through The Looking-Glass: A Musical Vaudeville Stage Play, eBook ISBN: 978-0-9957479-5-1 and paperback ISBN: 978-0-9957479-4-4

www.ingramcontent.com/pod-product-compliance
Lightning Source LLC
Chambersburg PA
CBHW021023120726
47905CB00009B/3147